S.I.

MW00650913

THE LEGEND OF
LORD EIGHT DEER

THE LEGEND
OF
LORD
EIGHT
DEER

AN EPIC
OF ANCIENT
MEXICO

Retold and Illustrated by

JOHN M.D. POHL

OXFORD
UNIVERSITY PRESS

For Georganne

OXFORD
UNIVERSITY PRESS

Oxford   New York

Athens Auckland Bangkok Bogotá Buenos Aires Cape Town
Dar es Salaam Delhi Florence Hong Kong Istanbul Karachi
Kolkata Kuala Lumpur Madrid Melbourne Mexico City Mumbai Nairobi
Paris Sào Paulo Shanghai Singapore Taipei Tokyo Toronto Warsaw
with associated companies in Berlin   Ibadan

Copyright © 2002 by John M.D. Pohl
Published by Oxford University Press, Inc.
198 Madison Avenue, New York, NY 10016

Oxford is a registered trademark of Oxford University Press

All rights reserved. No part of this publication
may be reproduced, stored in a retrieval system, or transmitted,
in any form or by any means, electronic, mechanical,
photocopying, recording, or otherwise, without the prior
permission of Oxford University Press.

Library of Congress Cataloging-in-Publication Data
Pohl, John M. D.
The legend of Lord Eight Deer : an epic of ancient Mexico / retold and illustrated by John M. D. Pohl.
p. cm.
Summary: Relates the tale of a powerful conqueror and hero who ruled over the
Mixtec people of the Mexican state of Oaxaca between 1063 and 1115. Includes information
on how the codices containing the story were deciphered.

ISBN 0-19-514019-2 (lib. bdg.) – ISBN 0-19-514020-6

1. Mixtec Indians—Folklore. 2. Mixtec Indians—Kings and rulers—Juvenile literature. 3. Legends—Mexico.
[1. Mixtec Indians—Folklore 2. Indians of Mexico—Folklore. 3. Folklore—Mexico.] I. Title.

F1219.8.M59 P65 2001
398.2'089'97—dc21   2001031406

9 8 7 6 5 4 3 2 1

Printed in Hong Kong on acid free paper
Design and layout: Nora Wertz

*The fine-art reproductions in this book were made possible by a generous grant
from the Foundation for the Advancement of Mesoamerican Studies,
to whom Oxford wishes to extend its appreciation.*

Half title: The place sign for Eight Deer's kingdom of Tilantongo, which means Black
Town*; Overleaf: The Stone People rise up from the earth to join forces with warriors
from the stars and do battle with the kings of Hill of the Wasp and Place of Flints; Below:
Codex Zouche-Nuttall, British Museum.*

CONTENTS

INTRODUCTION: The War that Came from Heaven 6

CAST OF CHARACTERS 8

CHRONOLOGY 9

THE LEGEND OF LORD EIGHT DEER

   Eight Deer and the Priestess of the Dead 11

   Queen Six Monkey 17

   Eight Deer Returns 22

   Assassination 24

   The Ball Game 28

   Journey to the Oracle of the Sun 34

   Vengeance 44

   The Final Battle..49

   The Death of Eight Deer and the Legacy He Left........................53

THE STORY BEHIND THE STORY.....................................56

THE WAR THAT CAME
FROM HEAVEN

Lord Eight Deer, known as Iya Nacuaa in his own language, was a great Mixtec Indian conqueror and hero who lived nearly a thousand years ago, between 1063 and 1115. His biography is portrayed in the Mixtec codices, religious books printed on animal hides that contain the longest continuous history known for any American Indian civilization. The Mixtec people, over whom Eight Deer ruled, occupied the rugged mountains of what is today the Mexican state of Oaxaca. Thanks to the efforts of archaeologists, art historians, and, most importantly, the Mixtec people living today, we have learned that the legend in the pictographs tells us the true story of Eight Deer's life.

After 25 years of research, I have determined that the saga of Lord Eight Deer originated with a tragic dynastic conflict that I call the War that Came from Heaven, which began between the years 963 and 979. The war began after the lords of two prominent royal families ruling at Hill of the Wasp married princesses from Hill of the Sun. Apparently, these alliances upset a balance of power, for shortly thereafter war broke out. Soon it became a cosmic struggle in which the sun itself was eclipsed and the very stones of the earth and the stars of the sky were called forth to fight as supernatural warriors. When the struggle ended, all the male heirs to the throne of Hill of the Wasp had been murdered. Only two daughters survived the destruction of their king- dom. One princess married the king of Tilantongo, while the other married the lord from a neighboring kingdom that I call Red and White Bundle, a reference to a sacred object that identifies the place sign in the codices. The dynasty of the once mighty Hill of the Wasp was thereby divided between two rival families.

By 1041, Tilantongo and a third kingdom, Jaltepec, had allied their royal houses through two generations of marriage, leading to a period of relative peace in the region. War erupted again, however, when three princes from Jaltepec were mysteriously assassinated. We can only speculate that Tilantongo was to blame, for the Jaltepec king broke the alliance by marrying his daughter, Lady Six Monkey, to the rival king of Red and White Bundle. A young Tilantongo heir was later found dead under mysterious circumstances, thus ending the kingdom's first dynasty. Lord Eight Deer, the son of a high priest, usurped the throne of Tilantongo shortly thereafter. When the Jaltepec princes are killed, the legend of Lord Eight Deer begins.

CAST OF CHARACTERS

LORD
EIGHT DEER

Son of Lord Five
Crocodile, high priest of
Tilantongo

LADY
SIX MONKEY

Queen
of Jaltepec

LORD
ELEVEN WIND

King of
Red and White Bundle

LADY NINE
GRASS

Priestess
of the Dead

LORD TWELVE
EARTHQUAKE

Lord Eight Deer's
half-brother

LORD TWO
RAIN

Heir to the throne
of Tilantongo

LORD FOUR
JAGUAR

Leader of the
Toltec people

LORD
NINE WATER

Eight Deer's guide
on his journey to
the oracle

LORD
ONE DEATH

Oracle of the Sun

LORD
TEN DOG

Son of Eleven Wind

LORD
SIX HOUSE

Son of Eleven Wind

CHRONOLOGY

1041   Lord Ten Eagle of Tilantongo marries Lady Nine Wind at Jaltepec

1043   Lord Five Crocodile, high priest of Tilantongo, marries Lady Nine Eagle

1045   Lord Twelve Earthquake is born to Lord Five Crocodile

1047   Lady Six Lizard is born to Five Crocodile; she later marries Lord Eleven Wind of Red and White Bundle and has two sons, Lord Ten Dog and Lord Six House

1063   Lord Eight Deer is born to Lord Five Crocodile and his second wife

1073   Lady Six Monkey is born to Lord Ten Eagle and Lady Nine Wind at Jaltepec; the three sons of Lord Ten Eagle and Lady Nine Wind are killed this year

1075   Lord Two Rain, heir to the throne of Tilantongo, is born to Lord Five Earthquake

1082   Lord Eight Deer's father, Lord Five Crocodile, dies

1083   Lord Eight Deer, Lady Six Monkey, and Lord Eleven Wind meet Lady Nine Grass at Chalcatongo

1090   Lord Eleven Wind of Red and White Bundle marries Lady Six Monkey of Jaltepec

1092   Lord Four Wind is born to Lady Six Monkey of Jaltepec

1096   Lord Two Rain, the last member of Tilantongo's first dynasty, dies

1097   Lord Eight Deer meets with the Toltec Four Jaguar, who awards him the tecuhtli nose ornament

1099   Lord Eight Deer meets with the oracle of the sun, Lord One Death

1100   Lord Twelve Earthquake, Lord Eight Deer's half-brother, is assassinated

1101   Lord Eight Deer attacks Red and White Bundle; Lady Six Monkey and Lord Eleven Wind are killed

1102   Lord Eight Deer kills his two half-nephews, Lord Ten Dog and Lord Six House

1103   Lord Eight Deer marries his half-niece, Lady Thirteen Serpent, daughter of Lord Eleven Wind

1115   Lord Eight Deer is assassinated by Lord Four Wind

1118   Lord Four Wind meets with the oracle of the sun, Lord One Death

1119   Lord Four Wind meets with the Toltec Four Jaguar, who awards him the tecuhtli nose ornament

1120   Lord Four Wind inherits Place of Flints

1124   Lord Four Wind marries Lady Ten Flower, Lord Eight Deer's daughter

EIGHT DEER AND THE
PRIESTESS OF THE DEAD

In 1083, after the murder of the three Jaltepec princes, the Priestess of the Dead, Lady Nine Grass, called upon the nobles of the realm to meet at Chalcatongo, the sacred cave where royal ancestors made their wishes known to the Mixtec nation. The gathering included all the rulers of the great houses—the aged Eleven Wind, king of Red and White Bundle; Lady Six Monkey, queen of Jaltepec; and Eight Deer, who was 20 years old. Because his father, the high councilor of Tilantongo, had died the year before, Eight Deer had been appointed to represent Prince Two Rain, the child pretender to Tilantongo's throne.

At Chalcatongo, Eight Deer found himself seated before a host of the dead placed on the great scaffold. Each mummy had been dressed in a fine cape, their faces concealed by expressionless decorative masks. Eight Deer shivered when he saw the three new mummies, the Jaltepec princes, among the ancient dead. He knew what powers they possessed. No king or queen of the realm could rule without receiving prophecies from the ancestors, and only the Priestess of the Dead had the ability to make them speak. To insult her was to invite excommunication, the loss of one's land, and exile from the realm. Eight Deer peered at old Eleven Wind, knowing that he was planning to rob

Seeking their wisdom, Lady Nine Grass approaches a gathering of dead royal ancestors.

Tilantongo of its power, and then at Lady Six Monkey, who was seated at the other end of the chamber. Only ten years old, she was clearly bewildered by the scene but maintained an air of dignity among the attendants that surrounded her.

Lady Nine Grass entered the cavernous chamber. Lifting a torch, she turned to the scaffold and addressed the host of the dead: "Southern wind, breath of earth's being, take my prayers to the souls who feast with my brother the Sun." She offered bowls of food and drink to the corpses' withered lips as a light breeze blew through the cave, accompanied by the eerie tinkling sound of the golden bells suspended from the stalactites hanging overhead. Then the priestess turned and revealed her hideous face; the flesh covering her jaw had been stripped away, leaving her with a permanent and menacing grimace. All were unnerved by her appearance as she pointed to the mummies of Six Monkey's three brothers and exclaimed: "Most noble men and women, how do you plan to end this cycle of pointless violence that plagues your royal houses?"

Lord Eleven Wind spoke first. "We gather to hold high converse with the mighty dead, to decide a proper order of marriage, and to reunite our kingdoms with their blessing."

The priestess considered his words carefully. "It is Tilantongo that has always been granted alliances through marriage with Jaltepec. Now you propose that right should be transferred to your own domain of Red and White Bundle through Lady Six Monkey?"

"Yes, Priestess, Tilantongo's king is dead, there sits the mummy right along side those three boys he murdered!"

Eight Deer leapt to his feet. "There is no proof of that accusation!" he shouted.

"And what of Two Rain, the dead king's son?" inquired the priestess.

"We wish to make him our king," Eight Deer interjected, "and when he comes of age to marry Lady Six Monkey as the law has prescribed."

The priestess looked at the scaffold thoughtfully. "Indeed, the ancestors have already given me word of their desire. Prince Two Rain is the child of a courtesan and holds no rank worthy of ruling Tilantongo. The survival of this nation can be ensured only if Lady Six Monkey should marry Lord Eleven Wind of Red and White Bundle."

Eight Deer was stunned. "By the gods, Tilantongo has dominated these marriages for generations, and now you hand our divine rights to our most bitter rival?"

The priestess glared at Eight Deer. "Would you have your wishes prevail against the voice of this nation?" she hissed. Humbled, Eight Deer stared at the ground in silence. "The ancestors have other plans for both you and Prince Two Rain," said the priestess.

Eight Deer had every right to be disappointed by the pronouncement. He had been brought up to believe that power was his right. His dreams and ambition could have taken him to the highest rank of royal councilors and warlords. Now he found himself cursed by the judgment of Lady Nine Grass and could only watch in silence as this priestess took power away from Two Rain, and from him, and sanctified the marriage of Lady Six Monkey to Lord Eleven Wind. Eleven Wind grasped Six Monkey by the hand and smiled a devilish grin. She seemed none too pleased with such an old man, even though it would be years before they would be married. She glanced furtively at Eight Deer, the bronzed warrior of 20. She could not remember when she had not loved him, but to honor her father's wishes, she could not let him know it.

When the engagement ceremony was completed, Nine Grass summoned Eight Deer to her throne and explained what more she had interpreted from the voices of the gods. "You are to establish yourself as warlord of Tututepec, the wilderness land by the ocean, then you are to take command of an army and conquer the coast of the southern sea. You will prosper and bring us all great wealth!" she declared.

"But what of Tilantongo? It is my home. My responsibility is to Two Rain as his regent until he is old enough to rule," said Eight Deer.

"Two Rain will go to live with the priests at Hill of the Monkey," she said, "while your step-brother, Lord Twelve Earthquake, will serve as regent at Tilantongo." There was no arguing with the priestess. The warrior bowed dutifully and left to prepare for his departure.

When Eight Deer returned to Tilantongo, he told Lord Twelve Earthquake all that had taken place with the Priestess of the Dead. The two brothers were sad, for they knew that it would be many years before they would see each other again. Then Eight Deer gathered the Tilantongo troops who were to accompany him and said farewell.

"May the sun shed light on your path!" Twelve Earthquake called as he watched his brother set out over the rugged mountains. The little army traveled for a hundred miles over the treacherous mountain passes to reach Tututepec.

The Tututepec coast of Oaxaca was a hot, desolate country overgrown by an impenetrable forest of low trees, brush, and cactus. There were few sources of fresh water and almost no usable agricultural land. The nearest port was 90 miles to the east. Eight Deer soon found himself surrounded by many enemies only too eager to capture or kill him, and so he and his men set about building a fortress. Once the fortress was built and Eight Deer was secure behind five towering walls, he remembered the priestess's command. Reluctantly, he began a series of campaigns to conquer the surrounding chiefdoms—Hill of the Flute, Hill of the Snake, River of the Jewel, and a score of others. As if guided by fate, Eight Deer won every battle, and with every victory his power and fame grew. But Eight Deer was not only mighty; he was also merciful. He spared the lives of his enemies, thereby earning respect as a benevolent warlord.

By 1090, Eight Deer had transformed his realm into a tiny empire of villages and grand estates that extended for nearly 200 miles. Tututepec had become rich by trade and conquest. Having achieved great wealth for his newfound people in this way, Eight Deer sat on the steps of his palace one evening and gazed northward where the mountains of his homeland reared up through the red, windswept dust like some angry fire lizard of legend. It had been seven years since he had seen his home. He was concerned about the fate of his brother Twelve Earthquake, the kingdom of Tilantongo, and the dignified Lady Six Monkey.

THE MIXTEC NATION

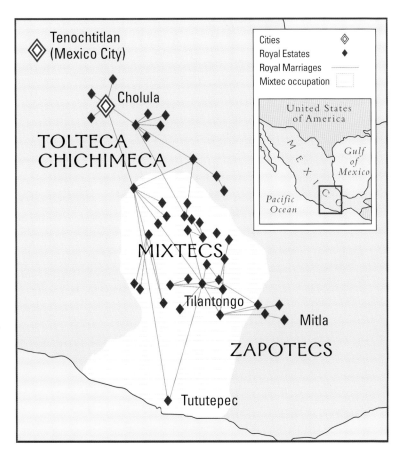

During Mesoamerica's Postclassic period (between 950 and 1521), the Mixtecs and their allies, the Toltecs and the Zapotecs, were organized into numerous small royal estates, each ruled by kings and queens who lived in palaces and formed alliances with each other through intermarriage. Today there are 400 thousand Mixtec-speaking people, most of which are concentrated in the northern and western parts of the state of Oaxaca. Their land is composed of a succession of very small, prosperous valleys surrounded by high mountains and deserts. Many continue to live in small villages farming their land much as their ancestors had for millenia before them. Others have migrated to Mexico City or the United States, where they have prospered in many ways of life.

This artist's rendition of how Lord Eight Deer, and other Mixtec warriors, may have actually appeared dressed for battle draws from representations in the codices and archaeological information about Mixtec dress and adornment.

A contemporary Mixtec family wearing the traditional dress of the community of Santa María Zacatepec, Oaxaca.

QUEEN SIX MONKEY

Six Monkey had just turned 17. As a child, she had been educated in all the manners and customs expected of a noblewoman. She quickly mastered the art of weaving brocade, creating designs of astounding intricacy. Before long, she became renowned for her skill in spinning rabbit hair into a silk-like thread and creating masterpieces of art that ornamented the richest palaces in the land. But fearing for her welfare after the murder of her three brothers, her priests and councilors now took the precaution of having her trained in the arts of war.

Six Monkey knew that to rule Jaltepec as her father had, she must command both respect and tribute from all of her subjects, including two rebellious princes living at Hill of the Moon. Her authority must not be challenged or she could be overthrown as rightful heir to the realm. She had to consider that the outlaws had recently sworn loyalty to Tilantongo, a hollow gesture meant to disguise their attempt to form an independent kingdom of their own. Although her impending marriage to Lord Eleven Wind of Red and White Bundle would all but reduce Tilantongo to the status of a principality, there was the pretender Lord Two Rain to consider as well as Twelve Earthquake, Tilantongo's regent. She could only wonder to what extent either was actually instigating the rebellion. The Jaltepec queen therefore thought

Riding on the back of her porter, Lady Six Monkey climbs the Hill of the Moon.

it wise to meet with the princes of Hill of the Moon herself in order to try to determine their resolve and end the dispute without bloodshed.

Six Monkey was bundled into a basket and lifted up onto the back of a muscular porter, her usual fashion for travel. The day's journey was short but arduous, and Six Monkey was looking forward to a rest. She arrived at Hill of the Moon early in the afternoon and dimounted to present her vassals with gifts. But the two princes responded to her offerings with insults. "Behold brother, here is the little embroiderer who would pretend to be our ruler!" said the first.

"I wonder if her weaving is half as pretty as her figure?" said the second.

Six Monkey was shamed by these remarks and shouted in anger. "Swear your allegiance to me or you will be punished severely!"

"We'll kill you...we'll kill you here and now before we'll submit to the rule of a seamstress!" shouted the princes in unison.

Although she was accompanied by her loyal captain, Three Crocodile, he and his men were hardly prepared to attack the palace, and Six Monkey directed her men to hurry on to Chalcatongo to consult with her benefactor, the Priestess of the Dead.

"Damn them!" cried the priestess. "Do they not know that by insulting you they insult me? It is time that you proved yourself a warrioress, or you will never be free from such rogues. Your priests have taught you well the art of combat. Now lead my army to triumph!"

Lady Six Monkey immediately returned to Hill of the Moon and demanded that the two princes surrender. When the first prince burst out laughing and mocked her again, Six Monkey was not afraid. She had already seen much of the brutality of war in her short lifetime. She immediately dashed forward with such speed that her poleax went hard through her enemy's shield bringing the man to his knees. The second prince was shocked and rushed forward, swinging his ax. Then, seeing the fearsome army that now moved into position behind the princess, he was struck with terror, dropped his weapons, and fell to the ground begging for mercy. Six Monkey knew that she must make an example of these brigands, so she directed her men to bind them as captives to be taken away and publicly executed. Then the warrior princess of Jaltepec appointed her captain, Three Crocodile, to rule Hill of the Moon as her vassal.

Upon Lady Six Monkey's return to Jaltepec, the people bestowed upon her a great honor for her bravery in battle. The priests dressed her in a new cape exquisitely ornamented with chevron bands signi-fying her prowess in warfare. Then she submitted to the demands of Lady Nine Grass and prepared for her marriage to Lord Eleven Wind. Though he was more than 45 years older than she was, he was the highest-ranking lord of the Mixtec land and would ensure the survival of her kingdom and her people. Eleven Wind sent messengers to negotiate the terms of the marriage with Six Monkey's council of

priests and elders. They presented Jaltepec with sumptuous gifts, from garments of woven cotton and feather to jewels made of gold, silver, turquoise, and jade. After days of debating who would inherit their lands and property if there should be children, the council consented to the marriage, and two priests accompanied the queen to Red and White Bundle. Eleven Wind had prepared a great public feast to honor the marriage, which was attended by no less than 2000 men, women, and children. There they pronounced Lady Six Monkey to be queen of Jaltepec and Red and White Bundle. Not long thereafter, Lady Six Monkey gave birth to two sons named Four Wind and One Crocodile.

THE TREE OF ANCESTORS

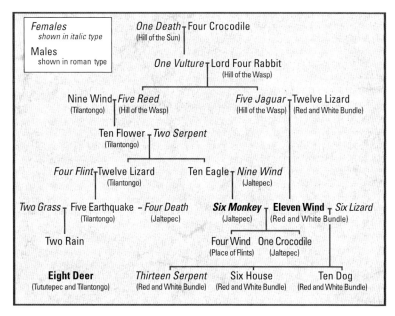

Females
shown in italic type

Males
shown in roman type

One Death ┬ Four Crocodile
(Hill of the Sun)

One Vulture ┬ Lord Four Rabbit
(Hill of the Wasp)

Nine Wind ┬ Five Reed   Five Jaguar ┬ Twelve Lizard
(Tilantongo) (Hill of the Wasp)   (Hill of the Wasp) (Red and White Bundle)

Ten Flower ┬ Two Serpent
(Tilantongo)

Four Flint ┬ Twelve Lizard   Ten Eagle ┬ Nine Wind
(Tilantongo)   (Jaltepec)

Two Grass ┬ Five Earthquake – Four Death   Six Monkey ┬ Eleven Wind ┬ Six Lizard
(Tilantongo) (Jaltepec)   (Jaltepec)   (Red and White Bundle)

Two Rain   Four Wind   One Crocodile
                                  (Place of Flints) (Jaltepec)

Eight Deer   Thirteen Serpent   Six House   Ten Dog
(Tututepec and Tilantongo) (Red and White Bundle) (Red and White Bundle) (Red and White Bundle)

The genealogy of the royal houses of Tilantongo, Jaltepec, and Red and White Bundle is plotted in this chart. These lines of descent sprouted from the marriages of the two princesses from Hill of the Wasp following the War of Heaven. Eight Deer started a new family line.

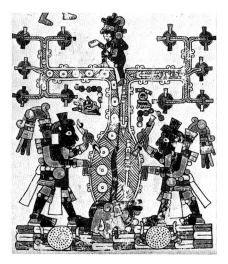

On page 37 of Codex Vidobonensis, the male partner of the first couple (top) emerges from a cleft in the tree that grew from the head of a goddess. Two priests attending the event carve signs in the trunk of the tree—arrows to represent man, and spindle whorls, part of a device the Mixtec used to spin cotton, to represent woman.

Mixtec nobles believed that their ancestors had been born from trees, a miraculous origin that enabled them to claim their ancestors were divine. Relating kingship to the gods, the Mixtec aristocracy had fixed their role as mediators with the supernatural. By having descended from part of the natural landscape, they could claim divine right to maintain land claims unattainable to the lower classes. Marriage was the means by which the Mixtec aristocracy enriched themselves, controlled their people, and linked their communities into political constellations. Because of this, the Mixtec were especially concerned with recording the genealogies, or family trees, of their divine ancestors in codices. By 1521, every noble house claimed descent from the epic heroes Lord Eight Deer, Lady Six Monkey, and Lord Eleven Wind.

In the codices, husbands and wives always appear facing one another while seated on woven mats or jaguar-skin thrones (above). Archaeologists use the term "marriage couple" to describe these pairs. On rare occasions, the codices depict birth. More commonly, children are found following the marriage couple as full-grown individuals, although sometimes a small umbilical cord attaches them to their mother (left).

EIGHT DEER RETURNS

When Eight Deer heard of the battle at Hill of the Moon and Six Monkey's marriage, he knew that he must return home to defend his lands and property from the ambitious Lord Eleven Wind. Leaving Tututepec in the hands of his ablest captain, he set out alone. After several days of traveling, Eight Deer stopped to refresh himself by a spring of water where he used to play as a child. As he knelt down to drink, he became enchanted by the sound of someone playing a clay pipe. Looking up, he saw a noblewoman sitting on the opposite bank. Eight Deer thought that a goddess could hardly be more beautiful. "Oh, that I could be the joyful subject of such a song of love!" Eight Deer exclaimed. The noblewoman was startled by the soldier's scruffy, road-worn appearance and called to her servant to drive the intruder away.

Late that night Eight Deer arrived in Tilantongo. His brother greeted him warmly, and the two shared a meager meal by the fire in the palace. "We are so poor now," said Twelve Earthquake, "that we can barely afford salt." Eight Deer opened a leather pouch and shook out a hundred nuggets of turquoise. Twelve Earthquake could not believe his eyes. "The stone more precious than gold! By the gods, you've come back to us a rich man!" Then Eight Deer told his brother about the woman he saw in the forest. Twelve Earthquake was concerned. "That was no ordinary noblewoman, Brother, but Lady Six Monkey herself!"

Although he knew she could be his enemy, Eight Deer continued to go to the spring, hoping to catch a glimpse of Six Monkey. One evening he saw her. He could not help himself—he was enchanted by her beauty and called out once again. To his surprise, Six Monkey sent her servant away and beckoned Eight Deer to join her. "I know who you are, Eight Deer," said Six Monkey. "I have never forgotten you, for you captivated my heart even as a child. How strange it is that we should still be drawn to each other. Can we really defy the will of our gods and ancestors?" The two sat talking, telling each other about their dreams and desires, promising to meet again. Before long they became lovers.

ASSASSINATION

In 1096, Eight Deer received shocking news. Two Rain, the pretender to Tilantongo's throne, was dead at the age of 21. His corpse had been found at Serpent River.

"No one knows for sure how it happened," said Twelve Earthquake. "They say it was suicide, an arrow driven through his chest by his own hand. Nevertheless, it was surely no coincidence that the body was discovered by one of Six Monkey's priests. You should never have trusted that witch, my brother."

Blinded by rage, Eight Deer ran to the spring. He waited most of the day, seething with anger. Then he saw Six Monkey. "To think I trusted you! You and Eleven Wind had Two Rain killed!" Eight Deer screamed.

"You're mad. He killed himself. My priest told me so!" Six Monkey shouted in reply.

But Eight Deer was not interested in listening. "Last year you seized Hill of the Moon, and now you kill the heir to our throne!"

Six Monkey winced, hurt by his words. "I seized the lands of brigands who threatened my life. As for Two Rain, he was never destined to be your king, and you were a fool to hang your fortunes on that bastard son of a murderer. Have you forgotten that it was his father who killed my own brothers and that even I have a stronger claim to your throne?"

Enraged, Eight Deer vowed his vengeance and ran from the forest. Six Monkey was stunned. She fell into the grass and cried, regretting what she had said because she knew she would never see Eight Deer again.

With Two Rain dead, Eight Deer realized Tilantongo needed a strong king. His own prospects for claiming the throne were remote. Without Nine Grass's blessing, who would support the claims of the son of a mere priest, much less the child of his father's second wife? The success he had achieved in life had come only through much struggle and sheer chance. Now there seemed to be little hope.

Then one day an ominous visitor arrived at Eight Deer's palace. He was a big, muscular man with a hunchback, painted black from neck to toe. Upon entering the court, the mysterious visitor raised his great red staff, pounded it into the ground, and pronounced "I have come to pay tribute to the great Lord Eight Deer from the priest Lord Four Jaguar of the Tolteca Chichimeca!" Eight Deer knew the Toltecs, a people who lived far to the north in the land of the volcanoes. The Toltecs were very powerful, and Four Jaguar was their great leader.

Eight Deer inquired as to the purpose of the ambassador's visit and discovered that Four Jaguar had heard of the death of Two Rain and the plight of Tilantongo. He wished to remedy the wrong that had been done against Eight Deer's kingdom and offered him the title of a Toltec king. But first he would have to endure an ordeal.

"And what is the test?" Eight Deer inquired.

The stranger responded "Lord Four Jaguar challenges you to a game of rubber ball, my lord. If you win, he will bestow upon you all the titles of a Toltec king and protect you from those who would seize your lands."

"What if I lose?" demanded Eight Deer.

"Then you must forfeit your life!"

It was all or nothing, but tempting nonetheless. Eight Deer knew that the Toltecs could turn the tide of war against any foe in the region. As things stood, Eleven Wind's ambitions clearly knew no limits. Eight Deer could soon find himself living in exile at Tututepec. The warlord thought of his childhood and how he and his brother Twelve Earthquake had played the ball game with such skill. He could have been a famous champion if he had followed that path to glory. He weighed the consequences and accepted the challenge. The game was set to be played at Four Jaguar's palace at Tulancingo.

FROM THIS WORLD TO THE NEXT

When a Mixtec noble died, his relatives carried out funeral observances with great rituals and feasting. First, the Mixtecs would wrap the body of the deceased in several layers of finely woven cloth in order to preserve it. They would then cover the mummy's face with a mask, often of turquoise mosaic, and place a crown on its head. Gold jewelry and other ornaments adorned the neck and hands. Next, the surviving relatives set offerings before the corpse and spoke to it as if it were alive. At midnight, four priests would carry the mummy into the mountains and place it in a cave. Each year from then on, the Mixtec would celebrate the deeds of their mummified ancestor on the anniversary of his or her birth.

A frightening Mixtec funerary mask magnificently crafted of turquoise and shell.

The Mixtecs buried their dead in natural caves (above); the Zapotecs preferred to bury the mummy bundles of their high-ranking kings in special tombs constructed under the floors of their great palaces.

This mummy bundle of a Mixtec priest was found in Coixtlahuaca below a patio floor. Because priests were sworn to poverty, the corpse was wrapped in simple grass mats and a plain wooden mask ornamented the face. Dishes and drinking vessels allowed the deceased to participate in the feasts of both his ancestors and his descendants even in his afterlife.

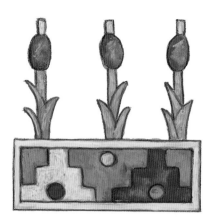

THE BALL GAME

The ancient Mixtec ball game was something like today's game of American football, though the players could not use their hands. They had to keep a solid rubber ball in the air at all times by hitting it with either their shoulders and hips, or with a special gauntlet in the form of a jaguar paw. It was played either one-on-one, or with teams of up to ten players on a side. When one side allowed the ball to fall to the ground and roll out of bounds, referees standing on either side of the court marked the territory that was lost to the opposition and the game began again. A match was lost when one team no longer had enough room to maneuver and gave up, which is to say they had lost all their territory. The festivities surrounding the games bordered on social mania, with kings and queens wagering entire fortunes on the outcome of a single game.

Eight Deer sized up his opponent standing at the opposite end of the ball court. Four Jaguar was fearsome-looking, with an oversize nose and close-set eyes. He had painted his body with long, thin red stripes that looked like blood. All around him stood high-ranking nobles wearing robes of scarlet, purple, and blue. Many sported outrageous displays of jewelry and had their noses pierced with amber, crystal, and turquoise ornaments, while the women wore embroidered capes of rabbit fur. Their faces were painted yellow and their hair was dyed dark blue or purple.

Suddenly, the 10-pound rubber ball fell into the center of the court

Eight Deer faces Four Jaguar in a game of rubber ball.

with a loud thump. The assembled nobles leapt to their feet, shouting as Four Jaguar ran forward and struck the ball with a leather mit, sending it flying back up into the sky. Eight Deer raced backward to receive, but it was too late. The ball hit the ground with a crack and rolled out of bounds. A referee ran to the center of the court and announced: "And Four Jaguar wins the point!"

Eight Deer was sweating profusely as he glanced over his shoulder at the burly executioner standing behind him. Hisses and boos from the Tilantongo side of the court sent the referee scurrying over to the Tulancingo sideline. As the match proceeded throughout the day, Eight Deer realized that Four Jaguar was a tougher opponent than he had anticipated.

The final round of the match began when Four Jaguar rebounded a low ball off the flat, round stone in the center of the court. Eight Deer fell to his knees and rolled beneath the ball, striking hard with his thigh. The ball bounced back up into the air toward Four Jaguar, and the fierce round of volleying began once again. Fighting for his life, Eight Deer mustered his last reserves of strength and slowly, relentlessly, drove Four Jaguar into his own end zone. Left with no room to maneuver, the Toltec lord made one last attempt to return the ball. He failed.

When the ball passed out of reach and rolled dead to the ground, chaos broke out among the guests; they overturned benches and threw their drinks to the ground. Many would lose a fortune in wagers that day. Accusations of cheating were followed by a good round of insults between the Tilantongo and Tulancingo factions until armed men surrounded the court and the referees called a halt to the fighting. Four Jaguar got to his feet, lifted Eight Deer off the ground, embraced him, and announced to all who attended the competition, "this is a most worthy opponent. Now we will feast in honor of his victory!"

Exotic delights were set out on woven mats across the center of the patio of Four Jaguar's palace: platters of white tamales formed like sea shells, turkey smothered in a spicy chocolate sauce called mole, rabbit baked in ground squash seeds and tomatoes. The food was exquisite, but Eight Deer

RITUAL DRESS AND PERSONAL ADORNMENT

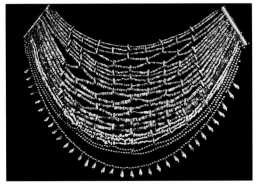

Crown and necklace: The Mixtec nobility used ornaments and jewelry to convey their identity, wealth, and privileged status in society. A golden headdress and a necklace of gold, turquoise, and shell found in Tomb 7 at Monte Alban were intended to project power.

Lip ornament: Crafted from gold, this snake-like piece of jewelry would have been inserted into the wearer's lower lip. The tongue was fixed on a hinge and wiggled as the wearer spoke.

Clothing and personal adornment served as more than just symbols of prestige. They functioned as gifts that confirmed agreements between nobles. As the Mixtec competed fiercely at gift giving in order to cement marriages, many realized that the greater a royal house's ability to acquire exotic materials and craft them into jewels, textiles, and featherwork, the better marriages they could negotiate. With better marriages, a royal house could attain a higher rank within an alliance network. Turquoise, imported through Tututepec from the American Southwest, was used with amber and shell to create beautiful necklaces as well as intricate mosaic sculptures. The long, shimmering green plumes of the quetzal bird from Guatemala were highly prized for headdresses and back ornaments. When gold was discovered in the mountains south of Jaltepec, royal artisans crafted it into works of astounding design.

Pendant: Found at Yanhuitlan, Oaxaca, this gold and turquoise chest piece shows the exquisite metalworking abilities of Mixtec artisans.

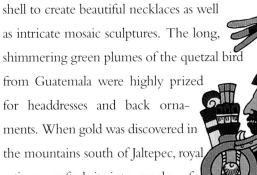

Skull: This human skull, painted black and red and encrusted with shell, was most likely worn on a belt at the middle of the back, as demonstrated by Lord Eight Deer in the Codex Zouche-Nuttall.

was so exhausted that he could hardly eat. He sat sipping a fermented wine called octli and thought about how lucky he had been as he listened to the sounds of laughter and delight. He had his brother to thank for teaching him to play the ball game so well; who would have thought all those many years ago that he would have to defend his very life with such a skill. After many hours of drinking and eating, the guests had settled their debts amicably and began to retire. Then Four Jaguar sat down beside Eight Deer "You've proven that you are ready to forfeit your life to defend your kingdom, but what can you show us of your military prowess?" he asked.

Eight Deer swallowed the last few drops of octli remaining in his goblet, pondered a moment, and then responded. "I'll go to the Hill of the Moon and return in three days with a gift of proper military tribute."

At dawn, Eight Deer set off with his men to attack the fortress held by Six Monkey's vassal. The fight was brief but vicious. Abandoned by his terrified men, Lord Three Crocodile was promptly captured and sent to Four Jaguar. The Toltec was very pleased, and he fixed the date for Eight Deer's initiation as a tecuhtli, the designated patriarch of a royal Toltec family, as he had promised.

On the day called One Wind in the year 1097, Eight Deer stood at the foot of the Temple of the Plumed Serpent and gazed upward at the assembly of Toltec priests who awaited him. He had spent many days and nights fasting and performing penance before the images of their gods. Now he was prepared to receive the high honors that would empower him as a rightful king among them. Musicians performed a solemn tune with flutes and drums as Eight Deer mounted the temple staircase. When he reached the summit, he was led to a throne covered with jaguar skin and directed to sit down and lean his head backward. Four Jaguar then applied a long needle made of jaguar bone above his right nostril and drove it hard through the cartilage. Eight Deer winced, but the priest pinched the wound to stop the flow of blood. Then Four Jaguar carefully worked the pin of a shimmering turquoise jewel through the incision and fastened it above the left nostril. Though momentarily blinded by the searing pain, the new king could hear the cheers of his men all around him.

The Toltecs award Lord Eight Deer the tecuhtli nose ornament.

JOURNEY TO THE
ORACLE OF THE SUN

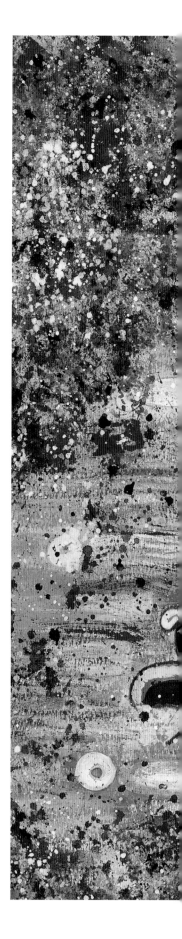

Eight Deer returned to Tilantongo after his time with the Toltecs, where he received the tribute of more than a hundred ambassadors representing kingdoms from throughout Mexico's southern highlands. Each bowed as Tilantongo's new king took his place on a throne carved from a boulder of solid bedrock set into the middle of the palace court. With his brother Twelve Earthquake beside him, Eight Deer addressed the throng. "You have made me king of this venerable house. May its ancestors now grant me the wisdom and knowledge to lead it to greatness!"

The ambassadors rose and shouted in unison. "You hold great wealth and power in your hands; it is yours to give strength to us all. We give you thanks and we praise the majesty of your name, Lord Eight Deer. May you be exalted for eternity!"

Eight Deer then walked among them and expressed his gratitude personally by distributing many gifts of gold and turquoise jewels, part of the extraordinary riches he had secured from trading on the coast of the south sea. "These jewels represent power, and power is to be

The three warlords, guided by Lord Nine Water, make their way toward the oracle of the sun.

desired! Now great lords, join me for my feast!" The ambassadors spent many days partaking of Tilantongo's hospitality, and each departed well rewarded for his pledge of loyalty.

Four Jaguar proposed yet another bold plan to Eight Deer. "I have made you a king among the Toltecs, Eight Deer, but I can never bestow upon you the title you need to declare yourself the divine founder of a new Mixtec lineage."

Eight Deer only laughed. "Ha! The Priestess of the Dead will never recognize any claim of mine over that of Eleven Wind or even Six Monkey."

"But there is another, more powerful than she, who can bestow the honor," added Twelve Earthquake.

Eight Deer thought a moment. He knew that his brother was alluding to the great priest One Death, the divine incarnation of Father Sun himself. "They say he can only be reached by crossing a great river that divides the world of the living from the world of the dead."

"It is a dangerous journey, but remember, anything worthwhile is achieved only at a price, and there is always suffering when one's life is gambled," said Four Jaguar.

The three warlords set out on the path of conquest. Together they attacked towns and captured many noblemen, from each of whom they demanded: "Show us the way to One Death, the oracle of Father Sun!"

But few could do more than say. "noble conquerors, all that I have is yours, but as for Lord One Death....I only know that he rules in a land beyond time, beyond space."

After many weeks of searching, Eight Deer, Four Jaguar, and Twelve Earthquake were finally met by Lord Nine Water, the prince of Sparrow Mountain. "I have heard there is a House of the Sun at Achiutla, but no one living has ever looked upon the face of One Death. He is protected by the spirits of those who fought in the War that Came from Heaven. I can take you to the river that divides the living from the dead, but I must warn you that if we venture beyond, we enter the heart of the earth itself."

The warlords were undaunted. When they arrived at the bank of the river, they launched canoes into the swift current. Eight Deer marveled at the shimmering canyon walls. At times it seemed as if the sky itself were set upon the pillars of stone that arched overhead, but soon the river was roaring so loudly that the men were afraid and their hands nearly dropped from their paddles. It seemed as if the canoes would shake to pieces on the seething torrents, but Nine Water urged them on and told them how to steer. Twelve Earthquake came very close to being sucked down into a whirlpool that suddenly exploded up from the depths, spraying foam to the very tops of the cliffs. Then Eight Deer shouted and pointed to the mouth of a great cave looming out of the opposite bank, The men steered toward it.

Once they passed through the cave's gaping jaws, the water became very dark and still, like the surface of an obsidian mirror. Daylight gave way to blackness and bitter cold. "Deep are the caverns that lie beneath this mountain, for this is the path by which the sun returns to the east," cried Nine Water. The sound of his voice echoed off the looming stalagmites, great spouts of water frozen in eternity. Eight Deer could just make out a tiny speck of light ahead, and soon the cavern began to open itself up to a burning golden light. As the men continued to paddle, they were astounded by what they saw. All around them grew fruit trees shimmering in brilliant colors of yellow, orange, and red. There were flowers everywhere, and the air was intoxicating with their perfume. Looming above this sacred grove was a great blue palace that sparkled with precious gems.

"I fear we travel in a world outside human understanding," Four Jaguar warned as the adventurers dragged their canoes up onto the riverbank and started up the palace staircase.

"You do indeed!" hissed the voice of a shadow in the doorway of the palace.

"Show yourself!" shouted Twelve Earthquake, drawing his spear thrower.

As if in response to Twelve Earthquake's call, an army of monsters

Year Seven Reed, Eight Deer goes to war against Eagle Rock

Lord Eight Deer

Eight Deer's mother, Lord Five Crocodiles's second w

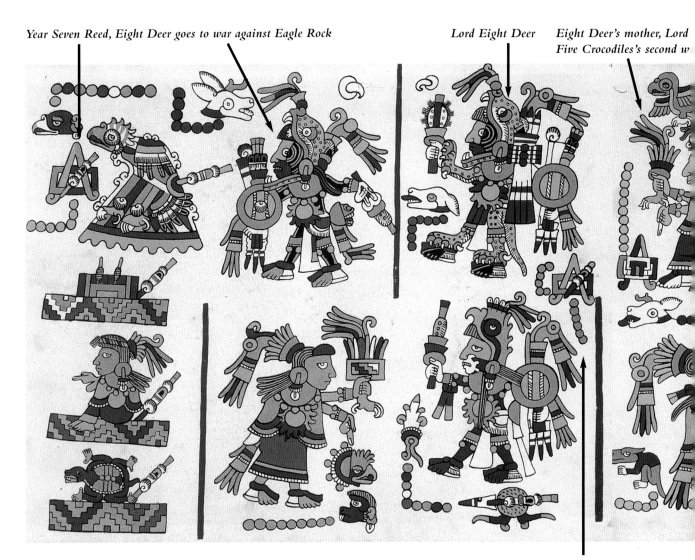

Eight Deer's birth in Year Twelve Reed (1063)

The Mixtec codices were made of animal hide covered with a plaster-like foundation upon which figures were painted. They were folded so that they could either be stored compactly or opened to reveal all of the pages on one side. The symbols in the codices represent people, places, and things organized so that they communicate religious stories, histories, and genealogies. The codices were not meant to be read simply as books, but could be displayed as "storyboards." A poet would recite the text from the codex to musical

Eight Deer's half brother, Lord Twelve Earthquake

Lord Five Crocodiles's first wife

Eight Deer's father, Lord Five Crocodile

Day Seven Eagle   *Tilantongo*   *Year Six Flint*

Pages 42 and 43 of Codex Zouche-Nuttall, preserved in the British Museum, detail the genealogy of Lord Eight Deer. Red guidelines direct the reader in an up-and-down pattern from right to left. Therefore one begins in the lower right-hand corner, where the place and date of the events is depicted. Moving upwards we see a marriage between Lord Five Crocodile and Lady Nine Eagle. Moving left we see Lord Twelve Earthquake, the first-born child. Below Twelve Earthquake is the second-born child, Lord Three Water. Moving left again we see the third-born child called Lady Six Lizard. At the top of the third column in the reading order we see Lady Eleven Water, who was Five Crocodile's second wife, followed by her son Lord Eight Deer and other children of the marriage. The account of Eight Deer's life proceeds in this fashion for the next 40 pages.

Artistic renderings of codices on everyday items, such as this scene from a codex on the pot above, reminded the Mixtecs of their history and mythology.

accompaniment while actors performed parts of the saga in costume. The setting for these literary and theatrical presentations was the royal feast. Imagine a banquet in which the participants were part of the art of the performance. They attended wearing garments painted with figures of heroes and gods while drinking and eating from pottery decorated with scenes from the codices, and exchanged gifts of gold, shell, bone, and turquoise engraved with images of the founding ancestors of the highest-ranking dynasties.

materialized at the summit of the great staircase. The warlords were dumbfounded. Many of the monsters were misshapen, even frightening. Some had no flesh on their bones and were little more than walking skeletons. Others possessed the body of a man but the head of an animal.

"Oh, but the living smell good. The scent of their blood makes my mouth water," muttered one hideous dog-headed warrior.

"Who or what are you?" shouted Eight Deer.

"We are the souls of those who fought and died in the War that Came from Heaven. Now we serve Father Sun," responded a living skeleton.

"Show us to your master then," said Twelve Earthquake boldly.

"It is forbidden. Only those who have died in some great battle may enter here. You trespass and therefore you must die!" The frightening horde moved down the stairs to surround the heroes.

The skeleton man charged first, swinging his copper-headed ax at Eight Deer's gut, but the warlord leapt backward, pulled the misshapen creature past him, and sent him crashing into a heap of bones at the foot of the stairs. At that same moment Twelve Earthquake narrowly missed losing his head to the dog-headed warrior. Four Jaguar was quick to strike that demon in the back, freezing it where it stood. A black slimy ooze dripped from the gaping wound, and then, incredibly, the spirit simply vanished.

The warlords fought hard. Possessing no living flesh, the souls of the dead should have hardly been a match for the warlords, and yet for each monster that they killed, it seemed as if two more took its place. Finally Nine Water and Twelve Earthquake succeeded in reaching the summit of the palace. They loosened one of the pillars that supported a beam over the entryway. Pushing the stone away, they sent the ornate stone facade crashing down on the shadow army, stopping their merciless onslaught long enough for Eight Deer and Four Jaguar to slip up the stairs to join them. Then Nine Water ripped a torch from the wall and tossed it into the loose thatch. The thick black smoke was blinding. The spirit army panicked and began to turn on one another.

"Now go inside, make your demand on Father Sun. Leave the defense to Nine Water and me," said Twelve Earthquake.

Inside, sitting before them on a great turquoise-encrusted throne, was One Death himself, his head crowned with golden hair and his red face shining so brightly that it burned their eyes just to look upon it.

"What do you demand that you would dare to make war against the sun itself?" bellowed the oracle.

Holding his shield up to protect himself from the intense heat, Four Jaguar spoke first. "You who see everything, you who know everything, we come before you repentant, but we claim your palace by right of conquest and now demand a favor in tribute."

"And what favor is that?"

Eight Deer stepped forward and spoke. "I do not defile the house of man or god. I am here before you to ask you to confer upon me your divine powers, Lord One Death. Reshape me, recast me a man-god that I may found a new dynasty for my kingdom."

One Death rose from his throne and addressed Eight Deer. "You vain and foolish man, do you not think that I know why you are here? It was my desire that you come. The fact that you and your companions even stand alive before me is testament enough to my blessing of divinity. But I will give you proof so that your vassals will know that you have truly looked upon the face of your creator." One Death instructed Eight Deer in the rituals that he must teach his people in order for them to properly worship him as a man-god and seek his blessings for eternity. Then One Death revealed to Eight Deer and

Four Jaguar three kingdoms reflected in a great hole in the sky. Two they recognized as their own realms, Tilantongo and Tulancingo. They saw that their people were happy and prosperous. The third kingdom they had never seen before. It was called Place of Flints. "It is only the shadow of some future event. It does not concern you now," said One Death ominously.

Eight Deer and Four Jaguar then left the oracle of Father Sun and found their companions keeping watch by the palace entrance. "When the veil of smoke lifted, the enemy had all gone." said Nine Water.

"But your face, Eight Deer, it shines, it radiates like that of some god. Truly you are now our divine lord, brother!" said Twelve Earthquake.

The heroes were grateful to Nine Water for showing them the way to One Death and rewarded him with a golden jewel. Once they had made their way safely back to the world of the living, they said farewell and returned to their kingdoms.

VENGEANCE

At Red and White Bundle, Eleven Wind and Six Monkey listened in shock as the messenger told them of Eight Deer's exploits. They could not comprehend how he had persuaded so many of the lords of the realm to accept him as their true king, much less the oracle of the sun himself.

"These Toltec usurpers infest our palaces like moths, slowly, silently eating away at our most revered institutions," brooded Eleven Wind. "Are you not saddened by the death of your own Captain Three Crocodile, my lady?"

"Not even a river of blood could wash away the stain of this disgrace," whispered Six Monkey tearfully. Eleven Wind decided to consult his eldest sons, Ten Dog and Six House. "Father, you should have killed Eight Deer many years ago. Now he and Twelve Earthquake have become too rich and powerful for you, and to attack we must adopt sham and trickery as our tools of policy," said Ten Dog.

Six House continued. "Twelve Earthquake is our uncle and he holds higher rank in that family than Eight Deer, who is only a step brother. Yet he has never married. Since our own mother, so long ago deceased, was both Twelve Earthquake's sister and your first wife, then it is we who should claim Tilantongo from Twelve Earthquake upon his death!"

"But Twelve Earthquake is not dead yet," said Eleven Wind.

"It so happens that we have just learned that Twelve Earthquake is sick with fever after his journey to the forbidden land of Father Sun and is traveling to seek a cure by purifying himself at a sacred sweatbath located not far from here. We have devised a plan," said Ten Dog.

Sweatbaths were very small adobe chambers in which a few men or women could rest, praying to their ancestors to forgive them for their transgressions and asking for a cure to their ailments. Attendants built a raging fire against the outside of one wall, and the occupants threw water on it from the inside to produce clouds of steam that were believed to cleanse the body. Sometimes the sick would gather bunches of special herbs and use them to strike each other lightly on the back, arms, and legs to stimulate the skin; they believed that the pores would open and release the fever into the air more swiftly.

When Twelve Earthquake arrived at the sweatbath, he did not know that the man who entered behind him had concealed a weapon within a bunch of herbs. As soon as Twelve Earthquake lay down on his back to pray, the assassin plunged the hidden knife into his chest, killing him instantaneously with one powerful blow.

When Eight Deer arrived on the murder scene, he was appalled, for he had dearly loved his brother. Eight Deer had his brother's body carried to Tilantongo, where it was carefully washed, placed on a scaffold, and burned.

"The voice of my brother's blood cries to me from this ground. It tells me that I must now find the courage to be evil just to survive," Eight Deer proclaimed. Then he directed his priests to collect the fire-blackened bones and bundle them in cloth. The next day a feast was held in honor of Twelve Earthquake's memory, and his remains were placed in a vault in the center of the courtyard of Tilantongo's palace. Eight Deer could never prove that Eleven Wind and Six Monkey had planned this insidious murder. But he didn't have to. They had both coveted Tilantongo as surviving members of the family from Hill of the Wasp. Now Ten Dog and Six House claimed that they should rule the kingdom as the rightful heirs of Twelve Earthquake himself.

Eight Deer realized that he had no other choice but to attack and destroy Red and White Bundle, burning it to ensure that its accursed kings and queens should never again bring such death and destruction to his land.

BATTLES IN LORD EIGHT DEER'S WORLD

War in the world of Lord Eight Deer was limited, practiced mostly between ruling houses bent on seizing one another's land. Peasants and farmers participated only because of the tribute they owed their rulers. Only about 10 percent of the population —males of a certain age and strength—were recruited to fight in the thousand-man armies headed by ranking noblemen. One of the ruling houses would declare war officially and determine a battleground. Since these wars were family disputes, sometimes the ruler who was defending his land found it more worthwhile to let his counselor-captains meet the aggressor. Battle lines were then established, and officers selected other officers with whom they chose to engage in combat as champions. The peasants fought among themselves.

Axe Head: When combat escalated, Mixtec princes discarded the atlatl and closed in on their foes with the deadly copper axe.

Mixtec Shield: Mixtec shields were beautiful enough to be works of art and sturdy enough to be instruments of defense. This shield was carved of wood, with a codex-style scene carefully inlaid with more than 10,000 pieces of turquoise mosaic. Feathers were once attached to the holes in the rim.

Atlatl: The codices show us that the Mixtecs preferred the atlatl, a spear thrower, to any other weapon. It consists of a pole about two feet in length that is designed to help a warrior throw a spear more forcefully, and farther, by increasing the thrower's leverage. Balancing a spear in the notched end of the pole, the warrior would grip the atlatl through the two loops at the other end. A man could throw a spear with at least 60 percent more power and accuracy using an atlatl than by throwing a spear by hand.

THE FINAL BATTLE

In the fall of 1101, Eight Deer marched out of Tilantongo at the head of an army of more than a thousand men. The troops spent the morning carefully negotiating the mountain pass, reaching Red and White Bundle in the late afternoon. Eleven Wind and his sons had spent many weeks preparing for this siege. Their palace was built on a narrow plain bounded on three sides by a deep gorge that descended some four hundred feet into the river below. Eleven Wind had to use his men only to defend his north flank, where he had directed them to construct an earthen wall to resist any direct assault. At 74, Eleven Wind was far too old to engage in any fighting himself. Nevertheless, he directed his servants to dress him in his armor. At the very least, his appearance before his palace might inspire his troops.

Eight Deer walked slowly forward to within an arrow's shot of his enemy's fortifications and shouted, "The man and woman you serve are bloody tyrants! Both the gods and those wronged souls they slaughtered fight on our side!"

Receiving no sign of willingness to surrender, Eight Deer then gave the signal, and the blast of a conch-shell trumpet sent his heavy infantry forward at a run through a furious hail of sling shot fire.

Lady Six Monkey struggles to protect her children during the attack.

Miraculously, Eight Deer reached the fortification unscathed and called to some men behind him to bring up a scaling frame. With one great heave, they threw the cane and rope structure against the embankment and climbed over to join the enemy in vicious hand-to-hand combat. Eight Deer used his ax to slash his way through the first line of soldiers and immediately found himself face-to-face with Ten Dog and Six House.

"Though you are blood of my blood, I'll slaughter you here if you do not lay down your arms," cried Eight Deer.

"If we are to be conquered, let a legitimate lord conquer us, not some base pretender!" hissed Ten Dog. He drove a spear straight through Eight Deer's shield as Six House swung a hatchet down, splitting Eight Deer's helmet in two. Eight Deer was stunned by the blows and collapsed to his knees, unconscious. Only the immediate arrival of his own men kept the two brothers from slaughtering him. Surrounded at spear point, Ten Dog and Six House were disarmed, bound, and hurried to the back of the line.

While some tried to revive Eight Deer, the rest of his men now moved against Red and White Bundle's fortified palace, using a log ram to break down the barricades. Once inside, they found Eleven Wind and Six Monkey standing in the middle of the plaza surrounded by their servants. "Someone bring me a pike or an ax that I may defend my family!" cried Eleven Wind. Exhausted and outnumbered, the servants knew their fate would lie with the sacrificial stone if they did not surrender. They sank to their knees and begged for their lives as the old king was dragged away to his execution.

Once Eight Deer regained consciousness, he mustered his strength and ran to the palace. There in the patio Lady Six Monkey lay mortally wounded, desperately trying to hide her children. Tears came to Eight Deer's eyes as he knelt down beside her, cradled her head in his lap, and whispered. "Oh my poor Six Monkey, what filthy victory is this that I have won? Now death sucks the honey of your breath away and I can never more hope to hold you in love's embrace. I am doomed."

Six Monkey looked up and gasped. "We have been unable to alter the destinies that the gods decree for us after all. The boundaries between life and death are vague; who can say that we may not meet again in the afterworld with our ancestors."

Eight Deer watched the life slip from Six Monkey's body. Then he took her sons, Prince Four Wind and Prince One Crocodile, by the hand and led the boys away from the palace.

THE DEATH OF EIGHT DEER AND
THE LEGACY HE LEFT

Ten Dog and Six House were kept as hostages for a year and then formally executed in military rituals, possibly to appease the gods during a terrible drought that plagued the land in 1102. Clothed in the white paper garments of sacrificial victims, the two brothers stood trembling at the center of the patio. Before them rose a great scaffold, extending like some extraordinary stairway into the red dawn sky. When the shimmering morning star ascended over a dark mountain in the distance, the eerie silence of the palace was shattered by the thunder of drums and bellowing conch shell trumpets. An old man rose from the gathering of noble men and women and sang a divine proclamation to the court from a book of painted pictographs. His recitation committed the princes to their fate by declaring the legitimacy of the great Lord Eight Deer, who sat silent, brooding before the palace entryway. Soldiers escorted the condemned forward to waiting priests. Six House was lifted and bound to the scaffold, while his brother was tied to a heavy, circular stone carved with the image of the dawn star.

A priest approached Six House and let loose a barrage of spears. Six House screamed and then collapsed in death. Just as suddenly, men disguised in terrifying jaguar costumes with razor-like obsidian claws leapt into the patio and set upon Prince Ten Dog, who was armed

Lord Six House awaits death while his brother Ten Dog matches Lord Eight Deer in combat.

with only mock weapons. The attackers engaged their victim in an ominous game of predator and prey, but after a furious gladiatorial combat, the exhausted Ten Dog fell to brutal blows.

Following the execution of his two half-nephews, Eight Deer made the kingdom of Jaltepec a tributary but allowed Six Monkey's children to live there in peace. In 1103 Eight Deer married Eleven Wind's eldest daughter from a previous marriage, a half-niece named Lady Thirteen Serpent, thereby uniting Red and White Bundle's bloodline with his own to create a new dynasty at Tilantongo. For the next twelve years, the great war lord ruled over a vast domain extending from Tilantongo south to Tututepec, only to die as violently as he had lived.

One summer evening in 1115, Eight Deer was hunting birds with Six Monkey's son Lord Four Wind, who was then 23. Although he had treated Four Wind like his own child, the prince was forever reminded that it was Eight Deer who had killed his mother. Determined to avenge her death, he arranged to have Eight Deer ambushed by an assassin hidden in a cave concealed by bushes. On his signal, the enemy ran forth to drive a knife into Eight Deer's chest so violently that it killed him instantaneously. Prince Four Wind held up a torch and knelt to examine the corpse, for it was hard for him to believe that the great warlord was really dead. He directed his servants to have Eight Deer's body taken to Lady Nine Grass, Priestess of the Dead, and placed on the scaffold with the mummies of the greatest kings and queens of the land. Angered by the death of his friend and ally, Lord Four Jaguar attacked Four Wind, but the two eventually reached an agreement.

Four Wind lived at a small palace next to the ruins of the more ancient ceremonial center of Place of Flints, content to allow Eight Deer's son to rule at Tilantongo. Four years later, he married Eight Deer's daughter and thereby united all of the factions born out of the War that Came from Heaven. The great celebration was attended by all the Mixtec men and women of noble blood. Everyone ate the most exotic dishes of meat and fruit and drank the most delicious beverages of chocolate. The singing and dancing lasted for many days, for everyone knew that this union would bring lasting peace to the land of the Mixtecs.

THE STORY BEHIND THE STORY

The Mixtec codices portray a world of kings and queens that is at once awe-inspiring, even beautiful, but also brutal. I have often wondered what these remarkable stories meant to the ancient royal families who so carefully painted and preserved them. We know that the books were sacred, that they contained messages of devotion for the mind and heart. They spoke to the heroic spirit of valor and presented examples of both good and bad conduct. The struggle of a man standing alone in the face of adversity has always been a compelling theme of the world's great literature; we see in the legend of Eight Deer that the hero pays the ultimate price for his ambition. Queen Six Monkey and Lord Eleven Wind also possess noble traits, but as with Eight Deer, vengeance for past wrongs, together with single-minded ambition, finally causes their downfall. Ultimately, the cycle of callous murder that characterizes this tragedy startles and may even frighten us—not so much through its graphic violence, but by awakening in us the fear of confronting some inducement that could turn our own hearts dark with murderous ambition and the hunger for revenge.

My own interest in the codices began when I was a university student in archaeology. Having once worked as a staff artist for the Guthrie Theatre in Minneapolis, I was always searching for novel ways to bring the past to life through dramatic or artistic reconstructions. I was attracted to the potential of motion pictures and thought that the Mixtec pictographs were perfectly adapted to character animation. When I made a short film of Eight Deer battling his nephews and showed it to several experts in the field, I was dumbfounded to learn that very little was known about where the actual events took place. I decided to pursue a study of the Eight Deer saga for my graduate work.

It was the Mexican archaeologist Alfonso Caso who first proved conclusively that the Eight Deer codices were Mixtec. In 1932, Caso discovered a tomb in the Valley of Oaxaca that contained a Mixtec treasure of gold and other gems. Most of the jewels were magnificently carved or cast with figures recognizable from the painted books. Many years later, Caso published a landmark study of a colonial

Mixtec painting on linen, the Mapa de Teozacoalco, now preserved at the University of Texas in Austin. Caso was the first to note that the map depicted Eight Deer and his descendants through the time of the Spanish Conquest. He also spotted a place sign: a black frieze beneath a temple ornamented with stars, which represented a specific town beneath the heavens. A Spanish text identified the dynasty of the great king as that of Tilantongo, the common name still used today. Caso knew that the name of that town in the Mixtec language, however, was Ñuu Tnoo-Huahi Andehui, or Black Town-House of Heaven. The name fit the hiero-glyph in the map and the codices perfectly. The mystery of where Eight Deer had actually lived was finally solved. Mary Elizabeth Smith, who worked closely with Caso until his death in 1970, subsequently identified the nearby town of Jaltepec as the kingdom of Lady Six Monkey. It was the work of these two pioneers in Mixtec codex studies that led me to travel to the remote mountains and valleys of the Mixteca Alta to investigate the ancient ruins of the Mixtecs.

My first task was to decipher the names of people, calculate the years of the chronology, and identify the place signs in the Mixtec codices. I learned that people portrayed in the codices were named after their birthdays in a sacred calendar of 260 days. Each name was represented by a combination of 13 numerals and 20

Still buried beneath the earth of the Tilantongo Valley, the majestic homes of Lord Eight Deer and Lady Six Monkey would have looked very much like the surviving ruins of the ancient palace of Mitla.

day signs. For example, Eight Deer can always be identified by the image of a deer's head, the seventh day sign, and eight colored dots. Though many events are also named by days, the years they accompany are even more important for constructing the chronology of Eight Deer's life. Each year is distinguished by one of four year bearers—rabbit, reed, flint, and house—together with as many as 13 numerals as well. Because the Mixtecs continued to use their calendar well after the Spanish Conquest, we need only count backwards from a known colonial date through the generations to discover that Eight Deer's birth in the Mixtec year 12 Reed was equivalent to our year 1063.

I have spent many years since analyzing the sequence of warfare and alliance during the War that Came from Heaven and Eight Deer periods. Little was known of the locations of any of the other kingdoms, particularly with regard to the remarkable accounts of the War that Came from Heaven. Caso believed that Hill of the Wasp, for example, was some great Mesoamerican metropolis of more than 100,000 people, yet no archaeological site as large as that was known in the Mixteca. For me the codices were like a treasure map for an actual geographical space, yet for the most part I was at a loss to identify the ancient kingdom. Tracing the royal families of Tilantongo and Jaltepec back to their roots at Hill of the Wasp, Place of Flints, and Red and White Bundle, I concluded that the War that Came from Heaven and the conflicts involving Eight Deer were, for the most part, very localized. This in turn meant that the settlements represented by the place signs in the codices must have been relatively small ceremonial centers.

Together with my colleague Bruce Byland, I began to make settlement maps of the ruins around Tilantongo and Jaltepec. Initially we had wanted to survey the region if only to prove that the place signs in the codices applied to small elite estates and not entire cities as others had proposed. But before long we encountered many farmers who knew actual Mixtec names for the ruins as well as ancient legends. Some scholars think that Eight Deer may have proposed marriage to Lady Six Monkey. Indeed, he appears in the codices as if he were her consort. Others have speculated that they were lovers. One day I was showing my friend Don Crispín, who grew up in Tilantongo, a picture of Eight Deer and Six Monkey together. The story he told me was remarkable. "There was once a Tilantongo prince who wished to be the queen of Jaltepec's lover. The queen was very fond of him as well," Don Crispín began.

When the queen's suitors were unable to resolve among themselves who should be her favorite, the queen directed them to gather on a mountain, called

PUTTING THE PIECES TOGETHER

Using aerial photographs as maps, archaeologists plotted the ancient sites they discovered. They collected and dated pottery shards in order to determine when each site was inhabited. A change the archaeologists found in ceramic styles in the area that Eight Deer once inhabited suggested that between 950 and 1100, the once-great urban center that included Hill of the Wasp, Red and White Bundle, and Place of Flints (marked in red) was largely abandoned. Linking information from the shards with what they found in the codices, archaeologists have determined that the abandonment was due to a dynastic conflict that broke out between rival families during the War that Came from Heaven.

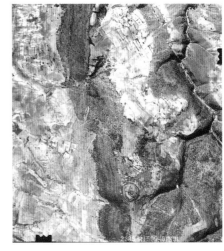

Aerial photographic detail of the region of Hill of the Bet and Hill of the Wasp.

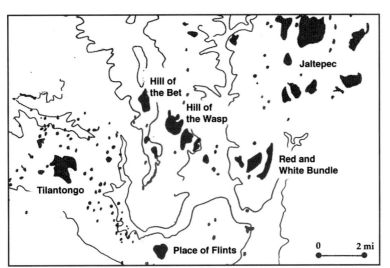

Pot shards from the Classic period (250–950).

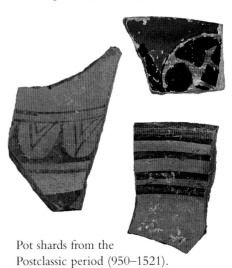

Pot shards from the Postclassic period (950–1521).

Identifying Tilantongo and Jaltepec gave investigators two key reference points for placing the world of Eight Deer and Six Monkey in a real landscape. Scholastic collaboration between archaeologists and the Mixtec people led to the identification of numerous other names for places appearing in the War that Came from Heaven and Eight Deer sagas. They bear testimony to the accuracy of legends still told hundreds of years after the events occurred.

the Hill of the Bet, where they made a wager that whoever could throw a stone farthest toward the spring where the queen was bathing would win. Each stepped forward and took his turn. But the king of Tilantongo was very clever. He had concealed a small gray bird in his cape, and when it was his turn he threw the bird instead of the stone. The bird flew those many miles over the valley to exactly where the queen was bathing. The others were astounded but still fooled by the trick, and so the king of Tilantongo won the bet and became the queen's lover.

The story fascinated me. Obviously, the people of Tilantongo and Jaltepec had been passing on an oral tradition of pre-Columbian legends for more than 500 years that was directly related to what I was seeing in the codices. Perhaps this was even the legend of Eight Deer and Six Monkey themselves. A few weeks later I made a second discovery that also supported my thesis when my survey team

Place signs:

1. Hill of the Moon

2. Tilantongo

3. Jaltepec

4. Hill of the Wasp

5. Red and White Bundle

6. Hill of the Flints

encountered ruins on Hill of the Bet and an adjoining temple complex. It was the temple complex that really fascinated me. I asked a farmer working nearby what he called the place. "Yucu Yoco, Maestro—Hill of the Wasp!" The name matched the place sign in the codices that marked the royal house involved in the War that Came from Heaven. Could this really be where the great cosmic war first took place? Excited by what the farmer had told me, I made a sample collection of pottery and other artifacts and hurried down the side of the mountain.

That night Byland and I examined the pottery collection from Hill of the Wasp intently. "There's nothing later than Classic period ceramic material here. That means that the noble families who first built the temple at Hill of the Wasp abandoned it sometime between 950 and 1000," Byland said.

My jaw dropped. That was precisely the time of the War that Came from Heaven and the destruction of Hill of the Wasp in the codices.

Now I was convinced that we were finding the actual sites portrayed in the pictographs. After three more field seasons of survey and excavation, Byland and I were able to identify most of the major sites involved in the War that Came from Heaven and Eight Deer periods in the codices, including Eight Deer's palace at Tilantongo,

Huahi Andehui
(House of Heaven)

Ñuu Tnoo
(Black Town)

The Spanish name Tilantongo comes from an old Aztec name, Ñuu Tnoo-Huahi Andehui, which means Black Town-House of Heaven. Archaeologists were able to link the city of Tilantongo from the Lord Eight Deer legend to the excavation site in this photograph when they realized that a place sign in Codex Zouche-Nuttall represented Tilantongo. The black frieze in the bottom half of the place sign stands for "Black Town," the place where Lord Eight Deer's palace stood, and the pyramid form on the top half of the sign stands for "House of Heaven," the pyramid-like structure in the background.

and later even the Temple of Heaven. During the Jaltepec survey, we not only discovered the ruins of the palace of Six Monkey but also other sites across from Hill of the Wasp that we believe are the ruins of Red and White Bundle and Place of Flints.

By correlating our archaeological dates for the abandonment of Hill of the Wasp, Place of Flints, and Red and White Bundle with the dates for the War that Came from Heaven and Eight Deer's conquests in the codices, an interesting conjunction in data has emerged. Both the codices and archaeological information tell us that before the year 1000, powerful centers like Hill of the Wasp were ruled by multiple royal families who administered their surrounding estates and the areas that paid tribute to those estates jointly. These families bound themselves together and maintained their privileged status through intermarriage. Eventually, the aristocracy became quite large and kinship relations very complex.

We know from the War that Came from Heaven story that different families then sought to better their rank by making alliances with kingdoms outside the normal alliance scheme. Unfortunately, this practice destabilized family corporate rule, creating internal strife, disunion, and abandonment. In the wake of the fall of these more ancient centers, the kingdoms of Tilantongo and Jaltepec ruled by the descendants of Eight Deer and Six Monkey then emerged to dominate the Mixtec nation for 500 years.

Today piles of stones marking the community borders between Tilantongo and Jaltepec are set upon the ruins of Hill of the Wasp, a testimony to the outcome of the War that Came from Heaven. Neighboring sites like Place of Flints and Red and White Bundle are said to be bewitched as though the very land itself has been cursed, even though some of it is the most fertile in the region. War was created by the gods and was therefore sacred to the ancient Mixtec rulers. They believed it provided the supreme offering: nourishment in the form of sacrifice to the sun, the rain, and the earth. But men and women, corrupted by greed and a lust for power, used war and sacrifice only to further their own selfish ambitions. Today the Mixtec people believe that the earth is sacred, that every hillside, every valley, plain, and grove has been hallowed by some sad or happy event in days long vanished. The very stones and dirt on which they stand are rich with the blood of their ancestors and their feet are always conscious of their touch.

Picture credits
All original art by John M. D. Pohl. Design elements by Nora Wertz.
American Museum of Natural History: 31 (top right); The Bodleian Library, University of Oxford: 21 (top right); British Museum: 4, 21 (bottom right and center), 27 (top right), 31 (bottom left), 38, 39; Donald and Dorothy Cordry, *Mexican Indian Costumes* (Austin: University of Texas Press, 1968), p. 261: 15 (bottom right); Museo Nazionale Preistorico ed Etnografico Luigi Pigorini, Rome, Italy: 47 (lef); National Museum of Anthropology and History (Mexico): 31 (top left and center, right center); Courtesy National Museum of the American Indian, Smithsonian Institution (10/8708), photo by David Heald: 47 (bottom left); Anthony Peres: 57; John M. D. Pohl, *Aztec, Mixtec, and Zapotec Armies* (Oxford: Osprey Publishing, 1991), p. 31: 15 (top right); Private collection: 27 (bottom right), 47 (top right), 59, 60-61, 62, 64; Michel Zabe: 27 (left), 31 (bottom right).

ACKNOWLEDGMENTS

I am especially indebted to my editor, Casper Grathwohl, for being so enthusiastic about this project from the start. I also want to thank Kathryn Hamilton for her efforts in actually seeing that this book came together in the way that I had envisioned it, together with Nora Wertz, who did such an excellent job with the design. I thank Carla Appel, Robert Williams, and Timothy Albright for their encouragement to even attempt a book like this.

ABOUT THE AUTHOR

After spending 25 years in southern Mexico, exploring the land that Lord Eight Deer inhabited and speaking with the people who now live there, John M. D. Pohl made the exciting discovery that the Mixtec codices tell real history in story form. Dr. Pohl is an eminent authority on several American Indian civilizations and has directed numerous archaeological excavations in Mexico, Central America, Canada, and the United States, specializing in the deciphering of ancient pictographic writing systems. His publications include *Exploring Mesoamerica* (Oxford University Press, 1999) and *The Politics of Symbolism in the Mixtec Codices*. Dr. Pohl works in Los Angeles as a writer, designer, and film and television producer. He is noted for his unique skills in bringing the ancient past to life through a variety of media.